'Timo Goes Camping

Victoria Allenby
Illustrated by **Dean Griffiths**

pajamapress

The publisher gratefully acknowledges the support of the Canada Council for the Arts and the
Ontario Arts Council for its publishing program. We acknowledge the financial support of the
Government of Canada through the Canada Book Fund (CBF) for our publishing activities.

Library and Archives Canada Cataloguing in Publication

Allenby, Victoria, 1989-, author
        Timo goes camping / Victoria Allenby ; illustrated by Dean Griffiths. -- First edition.
ISBN 978-1-77278-040-6 (hardcover)
        I. Griffiths, Dean, 1967-, illustrator II. Title.
PS8601.L44658T53 2018   jC813'.6   C2017-906449-5

Publisher Cataloging-in-Publication Data (U.S.)

Names: Allenby, Victoria, 1989-, author. | Griffiths, Dean, 1967-, illustrator.
Title: Timo goes camping / Victoria Allenby ; illustrated by Dean Griffiths.
Description: Toronto, Ontario Canada : Pajama Press, 2017. | Summary: "Nervous about his
first camping trip, Timo starts with a trip to the library to research canoeing, fire-building, and
navigation. But his biggest challenge turns out to be Suki, who teases whenever one of her friends
makes a mistake. Timo's anxiety that he will be the next one ridiculed threatens to ruin his trip until
a confrontation with Suki leads to better communication and consideration all around"— Provided
by publisher.
Identifiers: ISBN 978-1-77278-040-6 (hardcover)
Subjects: LCSH: Camping – Juvenile fiction. | Teasing – Juvenile fiction. | Friendship -- Juvenile
fiction. | BISAC: JUVENILE FICTION / Social Themes / New Experience. | JUVENILE FICTION /
Social Themes / Friendship.
Classification: LCC PZ7.A454Tim |DDC [E] – dc23

Original art created digitally
Cover and book design—Rebecca Bender

Manufactured by Qualibre Inc./Printplus
Printed in China

Pajama Press Inc.
181 Carlaw Ave. Suite 207 Toronto, Ontario Canada, M4M 2S1

Distributed in Canada by UTP Distribution
5201 Dufferin Street Toronto, Ontario Canada, M3H 5T8

Distributed in the U.S. by Ingram Publisher Services
1 Ingram Blvd. La Vergne, TN 37086, USA

*For Dad, who gave me
compasses I could hold both
in my hand and in my heart*
—V.A.

*To our old family canoe,
wherever you are*
—D.G.

Chapter One

"I have a great idea," Suki announced one day. Her eyes were shining like the summer sun overhead.

"Oh, no," grumbled Bogs. He flopped down across the picnic blanket. "I am too tired for one of your ideas. Come back tomorrow."

Rae laughed. "Bogs, you will still say you are too tired tomorrow."

"And the next day," said Hedgewick.

"That is true," said Bogs. "I guess there is no use in having ideas at all."

Suki smiled slyly. "But you will like this one. It involves you playing your guitar. You will be our Toad of Tunes."

"I will?" Bogs sat up a little.

"And it involves Hedgewick's cooking," said Suki. "He will be our Chief Chef."

"Really?" said Hedgewick.

"Yes, and Rae will be our Head Engineer."

Rae rubbed her snout. "I am happy to, of course," she said. "But what is your idea?"

Suki took a deep breath. "We should all go on a camping trip!"

For a minute, everyone sat as still as statues. Then Timo's ear twitched. "Suki," he said, "none of us has ever gone camping. We do not know how."

"Timo," Suki said patiently, "none of us has ever gone camping. It will be an adventure!"

Timo wanted to say that he did not like adventures. He wanted to say that adventures were messy and unsafe and not at all sensible. But everyone else was smiling—even Bogs.

"Oh, all right," he sighed.

Chapter Two

Timo was worried about the camping trip. He did not know how to make a fire. He did not know how to paddle a canoe. He did not even know what to pack.

"I will make a list," he told himself. But when he opened his notebook, his mind was as blank as the page.

"I know what I need," he said. "I need a how-to book. It is time to go to the library."

The Toadstool Corners Library was quiet and cool. There were rows of books. There were chairs in nooks. It smelled like paper and ink and comfort.

Timo took a deep breath and felt better already. He headed for the nonfiction section.

Sun and Storm: Understanding the Weather

Famous Explorers of the Ferny Forest

HERMIT HOW-TO

White-Water Wonder: Extreme Canoe Trips

SHELTERS TO BUILD ANYWHERE

CAMPING IS FUN: A GUIDE TO SAFE ADVENTURES

"This looks like the book for me," said Timo. He opened it to the first page.

TABLE OF CONTENTS

"This is definitely the right book." Timo carried *Camping is Fun* and his notebook to a small table by a window full of sunbeams. He read the first chapter and made notes about tying knots. He read the second chapter and made notes about paddling a canoe.

The third chapter began with a picture of a compass.

USING A COMPASS

1. Hold the compass flat

2. Wait for the red needle to stop moving. It is now pointing north.

3. Turn the ring until the N is at the tip of the needle.

4. Now...

   The N is pointing north.
   The E is pointing east.
   The S is pointing south.
   The W is pointing west.

Orienteering means finding your way. North, south, east, and west are called cardinal directions.

I do not really need this information, Timo thought. *I do not even own a compass.*

But he could not help himself. He made some notes about orienteering too.

Chapter Three

A few days later, the sun was just rising when Timo arrived at the river. His backpack was full of camping supplies, but his belly was full of butterflies.

He wanted to say that this was a bad idea. He wanted to say that they did not know what they were doing. But everyone else looked ready. Rae was tying two canoes up at the dock. Bogs was napping on a rolled-up tent. Hedgewick was tying a frying pan to his bag.

Suki was unfolding a map.

"I will be our master navigator," she declared. "That means I will show you all where we are going with this map."

Quicksilver
Lake

BEST CAMPSITE EVER!
Pender Pond
Ferny Forest
Toadstool Corners

Everybody crowded around to see.
On his way, Bogs accidentally stepped
on the edge of the dock. He stumbled.
He fumbled for something to grab.
He tumbled forward and fell against
Hedgewick's backpack. The frying
pan fell onto the dock with a loud
CLONNNNNNNG.

"Well, Toad of Tunes," Suki said with a grin. "I thought you would play your guitar, not Hedgewick's frying pan."

Bogs sniffed and picked up the pan. "This trip is already too exciting," he complained.

"Oh fuddle-feathers," said Hedgewick. "I have tied on that frying pan three times already."

"Let me help," said Timo. Thinking about the first chapter of *Camping is Fun*, he made a loop. He made a twist. By the time he was done, the frying pan was caught like a fly in a spider's web.

"That was some nice knot-tying," said Rae. "I thought you did not know anything about camping."

Timo felt a tingle of pride. It grew down in his toes and spread up to his nose. "Well, I have learned some things," he said. "I found—"

"Wait." Suki grinned. "I bet I know. You found it in a book." The grin became a giggle. The giggle became a guffaw. "You actually studied for a camping trip! You can be our—our—our camp librarian!"

Timo's proud tingle fizzled out. It did sound silly when she said it like that.

I hope I do not do any more ridiculous things on this trip, he thought.

Chapter Four

Paddling a canoe was more fun than Timo expected. He liked the soft splash of his paddle dipping into the water. He liked the *drip, drip* when he pulled it out.

Dip, drip, drip… Dip, drip, drip…

Paddling was hard work, but the *swish* of the water and the *shush* of the breeze were like music.

Then something changed.

The river became narrower. The current became faster.

"Watch out for the rocks!" called Suki.

"ROCKS?" cried Bogs. "You did not say there would be rocks!"

Now the river was twisting and turning. It bubbled and burbled. Timo wanted to say that *Camping is Fun* would call this "white-water canoeing." He wanted to say that white-water canoeing was not safe for beginners. But everyone was too busy to talk. They were gasping, grunting, panting, and paddling faster and faster and faster until the river gave a big *ROARRRRR—*

—and spat the boats out like two watermelon seeds into a wide, still lake.

"WAHOOO!" Suki yelled.

"We did it!" cried Rae.

"Yes!" Hedgewick raised his paddle in the air. "Take *that*, you mean, old river! Ha!" He was so excited that he jumped to his hind legs.

"Be careful!" said Rae. The canoe rocked right. It rocked left. Then it rocked right over with a *Splooooosh*!

Everyone helped fish Hedgewick and Rae and their packs and their paddles out of the lake. Then they were all ready for lunch and a rest on the shore.

"It is a good thing our packs are waterproof," said Hedgewick.

"It is too bad you and I are not," said Rae. She was using the tent poles to build a drying rack for their wet clothes.

"It was pretty funny, though," said Suki. She jumped up, waving a stick

over her head. "I am Hedgewick, King of the River! Take that! And that! And *wooooooah!*" She flopped onto the ground, kicking her paws in the air.

Timo wanted to say that it had been scary, not funny. He wanted to tell Suki that she was being unkind. But everyone else was laughing. Hedgewick smiled too, but he did not meet anyone's eyes.

I just hope that I do not fall into any lakes, Timo thought.

Chapter Five

That afternoon, the friends made camp in the Ferny Forest. Timo went out to collect firewood and secretly checked his notes from Chapter Four: Building a Fire.

Collect:
- Small sticks (called "tinder")
- Medium sticks (called "kindling")
- Big sticks (called "big sticks"?)

ALL STICKS MUST BE DRY

"That is not so hard," said Timo. "And the forest is much nicer than the river."

It was true. Above him, the leaves whispered quietly to each other. Around him, the ferns swished gently. Behind him, a terrible shriek cut through the stillness.

"Rae!" Timo cried. Dropping his tinder and his kindling and his big sticks, he raced back to camp.

When Timo burst back into the camp, the first thing he saw was a giant creature made of canvas and rope. Timo froze in horror as it rose up on its hind legs and waved at him with thin metal arms.

"Mmmmmf!" said the creature.

"What?" said Timo.

Across the clearing, Suki began to
laugh. Just then, the creature gave a big
shake and Rae's head popped out the top.

"What in the world just happened?"
asked Bogs.

"I was setting up the tent," said Rae,
"but the little pegs that attach it to the
ground are missing. I decided to check
the inside of the tent—"

"And then it all went *SMOOSH* and now Rae is wearing the latest camping fashion," said Suki. "Strike a pose, Rae. Tell us all about your new tent dress."

Timo wanted to say that it was not nice to make fun of someone for being squashed by a tent. He wanted to say that Suki was the one who forgot to pack the pegs. But everyone else was chuckling. Rae smiled too, but her shoulders sagged a little. "I would rather find some strong, little sticks to use as pegs," she said.

"I know where to find some," said Timo. He hurried back into the forest before anyone could tease him for being afraid of a tent monster.

Chapter Six

The first night was wonderful. Rae built a fire that snapped and crackled. Hedgewick cooked a meal that sizzled and spat. Bogs played his guitar, and everyone sang to a sky full of stars.

The second morning was awful.

"Wake up!" Suki called, banging Hedgewick's frying pan with a spoon. "Today is portage day!"

"Portage?" asked Hedgewick. "Is that a kind of oatmeal?"

"It means carrying our packs and canoes from one lake to another," said Suki. She pointed to the route on her map.

"WHAT?" Bogs sat up in his sleeping bag. "You want us to carry canoes? On land? Through the forest?"

"It is not very far," said Suki. "It will not be so bad."

But it was. Timo struggled and staggered. Above him, the canoe was heavy and hot. Around him, flies buzzed and bit. Beneath him—

"I think the ground is getting muddier," said Timo. "Are we walking near a swamp?"

"There is no swamp on the map," said Suki. "Maybe it rained here last night."

Timo wanted to say that the skies had been clear last night, but he did not get the chance. Under his paw, the ground was suddenly soft. He tried to back up, but the canoe pushed him forward.

There was a loud sucking noise and a terrible smell. Then the mud swallowed Timo up to his chest.

"Help!" cried Timo. Stuck between the mud and the canoe, he felt like a very furry turtle.

"Stay still!" said Rae. She and Suki lifted the canoe off Timo.

Bogs and Hedgewick reached out with the end of a paddle. "Grab hold!" said Hedgewick. Timo did. "Heave-ho!" Hedgewick cried. They heaved once—twice—three times—and Timo rose slowwwwly out of the muck. For a minute, everyone sat panting on the ground.

Chapter Seven

Timo looked at the hole he had fallen into. It was starting to fill up with water. He looked at his legs. They were covered in mud. He looked at Suki. She was beginning to grin.

"Timo, you—"

"Stop!" Timo yelled.

Suddenly, all the words he had been holding in burst out like water from a dam.

"You keep quiet, Suki! I do not want to hear about how muddy I am, or how funny I look. I do not want to hear any jokes about turtle-rabbits or—or camp librarians! We only came on this trip because you wanted us to. We told you we do not know how to camp. How dare you make fun of us for being bad at it!"

Everybody stared at Timo. Suki's mouth was open in surprise.

"I was just going to say that you were right," she said quietly. "This is definitely a swamp."

Bogs and Hedgewick chuckled nervously.

Rae frowned. "Timo, have you been upset about the teasing all this time?"

Timo looked away.

"But everyone knows it is only in fun," said Suki. She looked around at the others. "Right?"

Bogs nodded.

Hedgewick shrugged. "Your jokes are funny," he said slowly.

"But they can hurt a little," said Rae. "Sometimes."

Suki's shoulders slumped. "I wish someone had told me before."

Timo said, "I wish you had asked."

They looked at each other for a long moment.

"How about this?" said Rae. "You can tease me if a tent falls on my head, but not if one of my inventions breaks. They are too important to me."

"And you can tease me for being clumsy," said Hedgewick, "but not for making mistakes. I do not like feeling foolish."

"Go ahead and make fun of me," said Bogs. "What do I care?"

"But Timo does," said Rae. "So we should all respect his feelings."

"I promise I will," said Suki. "Timo, I am sorry I made you feel anxious. You are not bad at camping, you know. And it is my fault you fell into a swamp." She unrolled her map. "Now it is time to figure out where we are. It is a good thing I brought this!" She reached into her pocket and pulled out a compass.

"Do you know how to use that?" asked Bogs.

"Of course," said Suki. "You just follow the needle." She held the compass flat until the needle held still. She pointed in the same direction. "That way!"

Timo smiled a little. "Um, Suki?"

"Yes?"

"That is not exactly how you use a compass."

Suki blinked. "How do you know?"

Timo took a deep breath and pulled his notebook out of his bag. "I read it in a book."

Chapter Eight

That evening, after he washed off the mud and put on new clothes, Timo showed everybody his notes from *Camping is Fun*. Together they set up the tent, collected wood, made a fire, and cooked their supper. Nobody got eaten by a tent monster. As darkness fell, they sat around the fire in peaceful, sleepy silence.

"You know, Timo," Suki said after a while, "you can call me No-Good Navigator if you want."

"How about Master Disaster?" Rae asked.

"Lost Leader?" said Hedgewick.

Timo scratched his head. He scrunched his nose. "Silly Squirrel?" he tried. Then he chuckled. "I think I am a no-good name caller."

"Well," said Suki, "maybe that is a good thing to be bad at."

For a few minutes they sat quietly and watched the stars wink on one by one. Then Suki said, "Do you know what I want to do next?"

"Oh, no," said Bogs.

"I want to go mountain climbing."

"I knew it," said Bogs.

"Do you know how to climb a mountain?" asked Timo.

"No," said Suki. "That is why I want you to come with me. You and your notebook." She grinned. "If there is one thing I have learned on this trip, it is that every adventure needs a librarian."